Dominated By Strangers 2

~o~

A BDSM Romance Short Story Collection

TIMEA TOKES

DEDICATION

To all my lovely readers out there. Remember, no matter what your dreams are (naughty or not), you have everything you need to make them come true.

If you love my writing style, please check out my other titles on Amazon, and follow me on my blog & website for a FREE pdf copy of Squirm Under My Watch, FREE Audiobooks, and other goodies, to say a personal thank you to you all.

I am also hosting a monthly signed paperback giveaway, with at least 2 winners each month. So, please stay tuned, and share the love that's deep inside all of you.

Thank you!

www.timeatokes.com

ACKNOWLEDGMENTS

SQUIRM UNDER MY WATCH

~o~

<u>RUBY</u>

Why the hell would you want to go hunting? Aren't you working day and night to save animals? Now you want to kill one?"

My so-called other half asked, not even looking up from his newspaper. Someone cheered in the background, and my eyes involuntarily darted towards the football game. How Carl could concentrate on both the telly and his daily dirt at the same time was beyond me, but then again, he had never given *me* that much attention. Thinking about it, not even when we first met. Is this what I deserved? But then I guess we choose our mates for a reason. God, I must have loved suffering.

"If you haven't heard, hunting is about so much more than "killing", as you put it. And besides, at least I'm not running around like an idiot, chasing a ball."

Of course, my half-hearted reply never registered with my fiancé, nor did the sarcasm in my voice. If I didn't know better, I would say that he was immune to anything that would hurt his ego. And that included me. I let out a frustrated sigh when he licked his fingers and turned a page. Just how many odd habits of his would keep annoying me for the rest of my life?

Or the rest of *his* life. If he wasn't more careful, he would quite possibly make the headlines of tomorrow's paper. Something along the lines of 'he was a dickhead, until his fiancée cut him up with a tablespoon', or 'sadly, the biggest jerk that ever walked the earth is now gone'. That, or else my whole life would 'rest in peace'. I wasn't having it. But what was the point in arguing? It was always like talking to a brick wall. What brick wall? At least something could actually bounce off of that, but *him*? Not a chance.

"I'm leaving."

No reply, yet again, just the silent shuffling of papers, and the not-so-quiet booing from the TV. My guess was that the fans weren't too happy this time, maybe because their guy scored in the wrong hole. My own sick joke made me cringe, but it didn't matter. As far as Carl was concerned, I might as well have left already. Or I could have been dead. The idea was bizarre and morbid, but sometimes I doubted he realized I even existed, if I'm honest.

~o~

At first I wanted to tiptoe outside in my flip-flops. Mission impossible on its own, let alone when my emotions were at ceiling heights. Huffing and puffing I slammed the door shut behind me, wondering whether Carl would still continue to read the daily paper or finally grow some balls and come after me, dragging me back inside caveman-style. *Yeah, right, I had better luck winning the lottery.*

The heat of the sun hit me instantly, melting my make-up, along with my skin. It didn't help to cool down my boiling blood, either. I lifted my chin up, as if telling the sun to fuck off (something I should have said to Carl a long time ago, but somehow the words never left my mouth). Funny, when it doesn't really matter, then we can be brave. And when it would? I shook my head, taking a step towards the woods.

The only time Carl had shown any kind of emotion was the moment I decided to buy this little cabin. Yep, he was mad. Now, to him, that meant that he pressed his black-rimmed grandpa glasses up his nose, looking at me sternly. He didn't say a word. In fact, he didn't talk to me for three weeks. But I wasn't going to back down, no way. So, in the end, I bought the cottage and he got to keep his newspaper and the finger-licking routine.

I wish I could say it was a win-win, but I was willing to make the sacrifice. Anything for my dream house, and fairy-tale environment. If my life couldn't match a princess's, then my home should, right? Even Carl's annoying innuendos couldn't make the gorgeous smell of flowers, the buzzing of bees and the feel of it all fade away.

I sighed heavily, checking my watch, hoping that it didn't melt along with my sanity. I was even afraid I might actually shoot something, considering that animals are less attentive during this time. I was going to blame the blazing sun for not seeing properly, claiming that was the reason why I never arrived home with a trophy.

Anything, just not to hear 'I told you so' from Carl. The fact that he was right about me not wanting to kill animals was beside the point. I needed to get away, and I had to at least pretend I was going hunting, because I knew it had a chance of pissing him off. Oh, well, never mind that it didn't work. I was angry enough for both of us.

~o~

By the time I reached my favourite spot beside a waterfall, I was exhausted. I hadn't walked for more than half an hour, but the excruciating heat took the better of me. Give me some rain, and I would flourish. I would dance, sing, even clap and jump up and down.

But the heat is something I can't stand. Luckily for me, normally nobody came to this part of the woods, so I could relax, and live out one of my fantasies. Carl would never approve. To him, sex had always been an in-out-in-out-puff job. He always said that I had as much time as he did, but I never laughed. It rather felt like the joke was on me.

I leaned my rifle against a massive oak's trunk, then wondering why I was so desperate for company that I would end up with such a moron, I slowly lowered my skirt to the ground and stepped out of it. I still cursed under my breath, but the magic of the trees and the intoxicating scent of lavender soon made me forget about my not-so-charming prince. I stepped out of my flip-flops, gasping loudly when the velvety grass tickled my toes. I didn't need a mirror to know I was grinning like a Cheshire cat. I was always in my element in Nature, it simply captivated me with its beauty.

With heart pounding in my throat I got rid of my thong, too. My 'I prefer animals to people' T-shirt and sports-bra followed suit, scattering on the emerald grass. I glanced down for a moment, grimacing at the T-shirt. I started to figure out why Carl came with the whole animal-lover thingy. Yeah, I worked at an animal shelter, so what? It wasn't like he gave a monkey's ass about what I was doing, when and where. Why care now?

A gentle breeze made me shiver deliciously, and I decided it was time I enjoyed myself. I mean *really* enjoyed myself. The way you can only enjoy yourself when you are on your own, lost in the middle of nowhere. Yep, that's how I could always *find* myself. The real me. The sexual being that I kept hidden, because Carl never wanted to meet her.

Oh, well.

I took the pink rubber band off my locks, letting my strawberry blonde curls caress my lower back. If I was proud of anything, it was my hair. Okay, that, and my silver eyes.

The only compliment I ever got from Carl concerned those two. I sighed, letting my eyes wander towards the crystal depths. The sound of water crashing against rocks, combined with the gentle humming of robins and a cuckoo, made me want to jump right in. What was holding me back?

Nothing, I decided, testing the waters with my left toe. It was cold, so sinfully cold, that I could feel my nipples harden just at the thought of it enveloping me in its silky embrace. God, how much I loved to swim. And there was that *other* thing I loved. I snickered, getting ready to plunge in, when a twig snapped somewhere behind me, and I nearly fell.

I had a nanosecond to decide whether I should duck and disappear into the water, or face whoever was behind me. Could it have been Carl? I wondered, but I seriously doubted it. This was someone else, and as my luck went, it was a guy, most probably. As if I didn't have enough problems already, now I was facing a huge dilemma. I was sure that whether I was seen naked or not didn't matter, nor did the fact that I didn't want to be seen. I was here, despite Carl's warning, and that was enough for him. How long would it be, before he talks to me again? Three weeks? Two months?

God, I nearly hoped it was him behind me. Mind that, even then I would have had to have that 'talk' with my man. Maybe there was still a way out. Carl didn't have to know. If I acted as if I wasn't stark naked, the other person wouldn't notice it, either. Stupid, I know, but really, I was out of options here. Sucking in a deep breath I twirled around. I was so not expecting what (or rather who) was in front of me.

This male specimen was simply perfect. His alluring bad boy charm was oozing through the ether. What oozing? He could have worn a neon sign saying: 'I'm the most handsome eligible bachelor in town, and you are in trouble'. Even if he wasn't available as such, I would have wanted to make myself available for him. I wanted to scold myself, to remember that I had a loving fiancé at home, waiting for me. Okay, he wasn't always that loving, and he probably still hadn't noticed that I was missing, but still. He was mine, and I was his.

But this guy? He was something else. What was it about him that took my breath away, without him having to say a word? Was it his long black hair that framed a perfectly shaped face? Or was it his chiselled jawline, or his arched black brows? Maybe his sapphire gaze that held me captive. I was sure that if I wasn't naked already, I would have dropped everything (including my jaw) at his sight.

Okay, I might have drooled a little. *Fine, a lot.* I mean, seriously, what a man! Compared to Carl's sandy hair and dull brown eyes, this guy was a Hercules. He reminded me of dark castles, vampires and the sort. God, I never even knew I was attracted to this kind of thing! Well, clearly, I didn't know myself as much as I thought I did.

Mr Long Hair cleared his throat, shuffling his feet in the grass. I glanced down at his black riding boots, then my gaze travelled up his shapely legs, clad in white tight pants. I tried not to look at his crotch, but he seemed to have noticed me. Or rather his dick. Very much so, in fact. I gulped, forcefully tearing my gaze away, concentrating on his shirt instead. Bad idea! The burgundy material was buttoned down to his silver-spotted black leather belt, letting me get a very good glimpse of his tanned six-pack. What the hell was he, a super model? Or rather a ninja, having sneaked up on me like that while I was... *Oh son of a...*

My Eve costume popped to my mind, and suddenly I was too aware of the bulge in his oh-so-tight pants. What if the guy was a stalker, or something worse? I was half-expecting him to say something, and yet his voice came like thunder on a sunny day: unexpected, shocking and electrifying.

"By all means, don't stop on my account."

The husky voice was accompanied by a cocky grin and I searched the horizon for my gun. I wasn't sure whether I wanted to shoot him or myself that moment. But the rifle was too far from me, and also too close to him. I had to be careful what I replied, just in case. Should I plunge into the water, or should I keep standing in this awkward position? Either I had too few items of clothing on, or he had one too many. For the life of me, I couldn't make up my mind, so I did the obvious. Shuffling my naked foot, I pushed around a white rock. Another bad idea, as I nearly lost my balance while doing so. Would he have caught me? Would I have let him?

"W-What are you doing here?"

I mumbled under my breath, suddenly finding the white pebble more fascinating than anything else in the entire world. It was so beautiful with soft brown lines and creases...

"Trying to capture all the beauty Nature has to offer."

Was that irony in his voice? Or did he just invite me for a waltz? I glanced up from my Sisyphean task, just to meet his sapphire gaze. His eyes were twinkling at me like gems. I thought I was going blind. Wasn't it enough for him that I couldn't breathe, now I wasn't going to see, either?

"I see. And have you found anything beautiful yet?"

Dumb question. His charcoal eyebrows shot up even higher, and his lopsided grin widened as he looked me up and down. I fought the urge to cover up my lady parts. I lost the battle, and he laughed as my hands shot out to save the day. The left to hide my erect nipples, and the right to mask the dripping between my thighs.

"Don't worry, I'm not going to jump on you, or anything."

Oh, you won't? Why was I so disappointed? Wasn't this what I wanted to hear? I tried to mask my disappointment, I really did. I don't think he believed me.

"Oh, that's great, I guess. Well, if you don't mind..."

I motioned backwards, hands still on my assets, hoping he would get it. Not that I wanted him to disappear, but then again, what other choice did I have? He was a stranger (a handsome one at that, but still a stranger), and Carl was waiting for me at home. *Carl, oh shit...*

"I do mind, actually."

What?! His voice startled me, and I involuntarily took a step backwards. The mystery guy raised a hand in warning, but it was too late. With a loud splash I disappeared under the water. The ice-cold sensation cradled me, and I didn't want to come up for air. But I was no little mermaid (unfortunately), so I had to face my fears and embarrassment. Well, at least the water was covering the parts of me I didn't want him to see. My lungs were grateful for my decision, and I gulped on the fresh air eagerly, momentarily forgetting about my predicament. But I couldn't enjoy the cool air filling my lungs for long, as a second splash sent ripples of water my way, and thus into my nose and oh-so-conveniently open mouth. I vaguely heard the long-haired guy from a distance. Wait, his voice came from closer than I would have liked.

"Are you alright?"

I glanced up, and to my utter horror, he was in the water, riding the waves in my direction. And he was damn close! For some reason I stayed put though until he reached me. It might have been the shock of the cold water, or fear that if I moved then something bad would happen (or something good). I wasn't sure which scared me more. He placed a steadying hand on my shoulder, massaging gently, probably in an attempt to calm my nerves. Of course he achieved the opposite. His black hair was now wet, so wet that it looked like liquid charcoal. Damn, he looked even hotter like this. How did he do it?

"Define alright."

He nodded, agreeing that I had a point there. He looked me up and down once more, but this time his eyes were searching for clues as to my condition. I sighed, waving his hand away.

"I'm fine, okay? You didn't have to jump in the water to save me, I can swim."

He didn't have to know that I couldn't think clearly when he was so close. Was it because he seemed to be so different from Carl?

"I'm sorry, I didn't mean it that way. You know, when I startled you."

It took me a few seconds to recall the incident, partly because I had better things to worry about. Like his burgundy shirt floating around him in the water, or his abs at arm's length. I didn't even want to think about what *else* was at arm's length. And I was naked. *Oh, boy.*

"It's okay, I get it."

He took a step closer, and my heart skipped a beat. I wanted to duck again, disappearing into the water. But was that what I *really* wanted?

"Do you?"

His question left me speechless. How could a stranger care whether I understood his motives or not, when my so-called other half didn't give a shit about me? I shook my head, feeling stupid that I even compared the two. I mean, how could I? I didn't even know this guy.

"You know what? You are right. I don't. And I don't want to. All I want is take a swim, then go home to my fiancé. He must be worried sick about me."

I bit my lower lip when the words were out, and a pang of sadness and guilt filled my core. I couldn't explain why, but I regretted telling him about Carl, and I also felt bad for lying. What was the matter with me? A pair of sapphire eyes stared at me for a long moment, and I forgot to breathe. Then, as if nothing happened, he shrugged his shoulders, sending drops of water around us.

"Oh, I see. Well, I will leave you to it then."

I wasn't sure whether he was referring to swimming or my fiancé, but it didn't matter. I lost appetite for both. When my mystery guy turned around, silently marching out towards the shore, I had to think fast. Was I going to apologize for being so rude? All he wanted was to help me, or so it seemed.

But then, who wouldn't want to help a damsel in distress, if the lady in question was stark naked? It didn't take him long to climb out, considering that we were barely in the water, but it felt like it took for ever. His too-tight white pants clung to his ripped legs, and I wondered whether he would look good wearing a plastic bag, too.

My guess was *he* would. For a moment, I pictured him in a similar outfit as the one I was wearing, and it made me break out in cold sweat. My nipples hardened some more, and I could feel my thighs moisten — and not because of the surrounding water. My inner turmoil however didn't let me say a word, not even when he gathered his things and glanced at me, waving goodbye. That was when I noticed the camera. Why didn't I see it before? Yeah, right, I was too distracted by his cute ass. I cleared my throat.

"Wait…"

That was all I could say, and already it felt like I was choking on my own words. He stopped in his tracks for a moment, but then he continued packing leisurely. He wasn't going to make this easy, was he?

"I'm sorry, okay? I might have overreacted. A bit."

Now this caught his attention, but I nervously looked away. His blue eyes were too intense for my liking. But it wasn't like I was hiding something, was it?

"A bit? Was that some kind of an apology?"

He raised a perfectly shaped charcoal brow, and the top-model idea came to my mind again. I pointed at his camera, and asked the obvious, cleverly changing the subject.

"What's that?"

Okay, maybe not so clever. His gaze followed mine, and lifted the device up, looking at it closely. A mocking grin was playing at his lips.

"Well, you know, this is an object you can use to take pictures. A c-a-m-e-r-a. It's a very neat thing, if you ask me…"

He couldn't finish the sentence, having to jump to avoid the pebble I sent his way. My aim was pretty awesome. I could have easily hit him if I wanted to. Taking advantage of his shock and my newly-found confidence, I placed my hands on my hips, lifting my chin up in defiance.

"And this was a pebble. A p-e-b-b-l-e. A pretty neat thing, if you ask me. Oh, and have you seen my rifle yet?"

His reaction was so unexpected that I left my mouth open. He just grinned, walked back to me and held out a hand.

"How about we shoot each other then? Me with the camera, you with the rifle. Deal?"

I couldn't say anything to that, just took his hand, and he pulled me out of the water as if I weighed nothing. But what surprised me even more was the fact that he didn't stare. He turned around once more, making himself busy with his equipment. I was standing in front of him, in nothing but my pubic hair, and he didn't even wince. If I hadn't seen his bulge before, I would have thought that he didn't find me attractive. Funny that this was my biggest concern right then. The cynic in me didn't rest, of course. As soon as I was on safe ground, I asked:

"Oh, so you would even take pain for me, huh? How noble, considering you don't even know me."

He replied without glancing back, and I started to shiver. His voice was deep, husky and arousing. Very much so, unfortunately.

"I don't have to know you. But I would take pain for you, yes, if that's what it takes to get a photo."

Oh, boy. Why was I feeling a tad bit furious that he didn't come back at me with the usual line? I was sure he would say that he didn't know me, but he would love to. But no, there was nothing usual about this guy. Not his charcoal hair that brushed his upper back, nor his sapphire eyes. Nor his manner. How was I going to stay loyal to my not-so-loving fiancé like this? I was sure I could resist temptation until this guy came along, but now? When I was sure he had something better to offer? Something I didn't even know I couldn't live without?

"So, is that all you want, a photo?"

I bit my lip, realizing that I didn't want an answer. Not really. Because what I really wanted didn't involve talking. What was happening to me? I took a step closer to him, lost in thought. He turned around too quickly, and I ended up falling head over heels for him - quite literally, as I ended up in his arms after losing my balance. Since when was I so clumsy? How pathetic – and yet, how convenient. His brows furrowed, and he pushed me away gently.

"What else should I want?"

I gulped, my heart plummeting to the sky.

"Me?"

I didn't believe what I just asked in a whimpering voice, and neither did he. He pretended he didn't even hear me.

"Do you want me to take a nude, or are you going to get dressed?"

Rejection stung. But I knew how to get back at him. I had never had my picture taken before. Well, not a nude one, that is. But an idea started to form in my mind. To hell with guys, both this and Carl. I'm gonna get the naughtiest picture I could dream up, and then I will say tata bye-bye to both. Sweet freedom, here I come. Without replying I turned on my heels, swaying seductively as I walked up to the tree trunk.

I could only hope that Mr Long Hair was looking. And I bet he was. I reached down to grab my rifle, careful to give him the best view possible. He had to know what he was missing. God, Carl had to know, too. I would go home and shove the naughty pictures in his face before I left him for good, but first, I was going to have some fun. I glanced back over my shoulder, fluttering my eyelashes.

"Do I get to choose the scene?"

He nodded, firing up the camera. I stole a quick glance at his erection, and smiled to myself. This was going to be awesome.

~o~

swear I could hear his thoughts as he was snapping away. Or were they mine? It didn't matter, they made my cheeks burn nonetheless. I positioned the rifle in between my boobs and placing my finger on the trigger, I looked up at my gorgeous photographer. Boy, I was enjoying this, but so was he. He hadn't said a word since our heated moment, and I wasn't going to push. I just did whatever I felt like doing, and he took a picture in every position. Now I was standing underneath the waterfall, letting the velvety liquid cascade down my body.

Lead by a sudden thought, I started to rub the gun up and down between my mounds with one hand, while pushing the forefinger of the other into my mouth. And I sucked. I think he hissed, but I didn't actually hear it from the deafening sound of water crashing against rocks. Another photo was taken, and I had a hard time masking my frustration.

Moving the rifle down, I aimed it at my pubic mound. Still nothing. He didn't even gulp, just continued to snap away. God, I knew I was going to snap soon, just in a totally different manner. I even considered taking him up on his offer and shoot his family jewels. That would serve him right. Too bad I had left the bullets at home. Another tiny detail I would have to account for, when Carl found out. *If* he found out.

But instead of shooting my not-so-charming stranger, I kept playing. I had to admit that being exposed like this made me wet. My inhibitions were slowly slipping away, and so was my reluctance. Moving the rifle up and down, I made sure it touched my sensitive spots. Every single one of them. Twice. I could even say it rubbed me the right way.

Closing my eyes was my only option, the feeling of being watched while touching myself was too overwhelming. I wasn't sure whether Mr Long Hair still cared enough to take pictures, but I knew *I* didn't. If he wasn't going to fuck me, I had to take care of it myself, didn't I? It wasn't like I could go home and ask my fiancé to do the job. He was probably still watching football and reading his newspaper.

Well, his loss. And besides, who said that this stranger's presence prevented me from living out that fantasy of mine? If anything, it made me more eager to touch myself. There was just something hot and sexy in the way the water caressed my skin, the way it touched me in hidden and long-forgotten places. I needed this experience every once in a while. And, as it turned out, it was an experience I could share.

I grabbed the rifle, as if holding on to dear life itself, wanting the oh-so-longed-for climax to take over, and I moaned loudly, momentarily forgetting about my audience. Up until the moment the gun disappeared from my grasp. I glanced up, annoyed, just to be welcomed by a provocative sapphire gaze. One that set my blood on fire, his desire burning deep in them.

That moment I was sure they provided a mirror image of my own lust. I inhaled sharply, raising an eyebrow. His ninja status just got confirmed. He took a step closer, not that he wasn't close enough already. He surely wanted to make the distance between us non-existent. Funny that a silly joke popped to my mind right then. I was about to blurt it out, but luckily I managed to keep it to myself. *I don't want anything to be between us. Neither our clothes, nor air.* Instead I asked:

"Enough of the shooting?"

His charcoal brows wiggled, and his eyes darted towards my lips as he leaned closer. I licked them in response, and he groaned.

"On the contrary, just getting started."

I waited for our lips to touch, and I was sure it was going to be epic. But alas, he had other plans. Before I knew it, his camera blinded me and I stumbled backwards, disappearing under the waterfall. I'm not sure how, but the brutal liquid carried his laughter my way. *Well, okay then.* I did the most childish thing I could think of: I refused to come up for air. Soon realizing this was the dumbest idea ever, my eyes began to bulge and my heartbeat accelerated to the sky.

I swallowed a gallon salty water, and precious air was slipping away from my lungs. Doubt filled me, and I wasn't sure whether he would come to the rescue this time. Was I stubborn enough to drown if he refused to save me? Fortunately he proved to be a gentleman, pulling me out the last minute. I was sure my face took on an unhealthy purplish colour as I gasped for air.

I wanted to ask him what his game was, why was he doing this to me, but I didn't have a chance. I guess he thought I needed mouth-to-mouth, because as soon as I was eye-level with him, his lips sealed mine in a scorching kiss. I wanted to scream, I wanted to tell him that I came up for air, not to be suffocated by a stranger's tongue, but the words got stuck somewhere in my mind. *Very deep.*

He kissed me like he meant it, and I suddenly realized that he was way overdressed. I helped him out of his burgundy shirt, and watched bemused as the silky material floated away from us at an incredible speed.

"I guess we won't be needing that."

"I guess we won't."

He replied, cupping my right breast and nuzzling my neck, while I fumbled with his silver-spotted black leather belt. His white pants swam past his shirt, and we both giggled. We wouldn't have that much fun hunting for them later, but then again, I had to explain why my rifle got wet in the first place, too. But who cares about the consequences, when a gorgeous guy is kissing them senseless under the most beautiful waterfall? *Yep, me neither.* He exhaled sharply onto my neck, sending shivers along my spine. Resting his forehead in the crane of my shoulder, he whispered:

"Aren't we missing something here?"

I furrowed my brows, then shook my head.

"Nah, I'm on the pill, so you can relax."

He chuckled against my neck, then buried his hand in my strawberry blonde curls, moving the other down to my left thigh. He yanked slightly, forcing me to look into his eyes as his thumb brushed past my clit.

"Glad to hear that, but wasn't referring to a condom. What I meant was that we should introduce ourselves, don't you think?"

To emphasize that introduction, he pressed down onto my sensitive nub, and the moon, the stars and all the constellations swivelled around my head. And here I thought guys just boasted when they said they would bring you the moon and the stars.

"Um, yeah, sounds overdue, actually. But if I'm honest, I would call you anything, if you kissed me like that again."

And he did. Oh, boy, my insides were melting. When we both came up for air, he whispered between two ragged breaths:

"Eric. My name is Eric."

What, like James Bond? *My name is Bond. James Bond.* I smiled at my joke, but of course, Eric thought I was laughing at him, so he quickly added, pulling at my hair gently once more:

"Now you will know what name to scream when I make you cum."

As if by command, my inner muscles started to convulse, and he chose that exact moment to withdraw his hand from my clit. I gave voice to my disapproval, but Eric only laughed harder. Very well. I had a trick or two up my sleeve, too. Taking a deep breath I dived, looking for his shaft under the water. I grabbed it with both hands, then moved them up and down on its length, picking up a leisurely rhythm.

I could almost hear his gasp, and I nearly choked when I spotted my rifle embedded in the sand. Should I just grab that and run? No way, there wasn't a way out of this. Before my air ran out, I made sure to lick the tip of his cock, just to drive him a tad bit crazy. It was a funny experience, his velvety smooth skin mixing with the salty water, but it was totally worth it. When I emerged from the waves, I wasn't sure which one of us was panting more. I shot Eric a cocky grin, licking my lips. He grabbed hold of my wrist, pulling me close.

"Not so fast, *Eric.* Aren't we missing something here?"

Confusion spread on his face, and I could literally hear the wheels turning in his mind. It was priceless.

"No, not really."

His smirk made me want to go back down for my gun, but splashing him had to do — for now. He chuckled, spitting out some of the salty water. Okay, he might not be a ninja, considering that he failed to evade my attack. He raised his hands in mock defeat and I supressed a chuckle myself.

"Okay, okay, fine, you won. So, what's the name of this warrior princess? *Ariel*, perhaps?"

He made me laugh, but I wasn't a quitter. I turned around as gracefully as the water let me, and headed for the waterfall, shouting back over my shoulder:

"Nah-ah, you need to earn that privilege. I will tell you if you catch me."

But of course, I didn't rush, remembering another joke. I giggled as I pictured the mouse girl telling the mouse boy before they played hide and seek: *'If you catch me in half an hour, you can hold my hand. If you catch me in fifteen minutes, you can kiss me. If you catch me in five minutes, you can do to me whatever you want. And now I'm going to hide behind the cheese'*. Since when was I in such a funny mood? I didn't care. Eric closed the distance between us in an instant, and I squealed as a teenager when he lifted me off my feet and into his arms, kissing me on the lips briefly.

"Will you tell me your name now?"

I shook my head, and he dropped me into the water. I wasn't expecting this, so it was my time to swallow and spit out some saltiness. But I didn't want to get back at him this time. I watched in awe as he ran a hand through his long charcoal hair. The rays of the sun made him look like a sinfully hot demon straight from hell. He could have been the devil himself for all I cared.

It was my turn to kiss him, pouring my all into that single motion, wrapping my legs around his waist. I heard him hiss, but he deepened the kiss, placing both hands on my ass cheeks and pulling me onto his cock. He was hard and thick, and I was afraid I was too tight from all those years of having sex only once in a while, but it seemed like he fit in perfectly.

His thrusts were tentative at first, but soon enough he started to set a more pleasurable pace. I moaned into his mouth when his cock rubbed against my sensitive spot, and my eyes rolled to the back of my head, the moon, stars and all the constellations returning once again. My knees buckled, and I held onto his hips with all the force I could muster, while my hands clasped around his neck. Lead by a sudden thought I buried my hands in his silky hair, enjoying the mixed feelings this was giving me. I never had sex with a guy that had long hair before, because I had always thought they were gay. *Boy, was I wrong.*

Mind that, I had never had sex in this position, either. Eric held my bum with firm hands, while pushing me up, then pulling me down onto his dick. He didn't seem to get tired, and his strength turned me on all the more. Another thrust, and even the waterfall couldn't mask my screams. I was high on his touch, and I never wanted to come down to earth. His cock just felt so right deep inside me, that I wondered whether there would ever be anyone else who could give me the same amount of pleasure. And I didn't even know him.

I glanced into his sapphire eyes, and watched as they turn a shade darker, taking my breath away. I clenched my inner muscles around his shaft, and he thrust deeper and harder, until I cried out again as he buried his face in my hair, shooting his hot load into my wetness. My knees gave out, and I just clang there, hugging him tight like an idiot. But he didn't seem to mind, silently caressing my hair. I would have stayed like that for ever, but reality kicked in. Something hard pressed into my tits, and it wasn't his cock this time.

I giggled as I realized it was his camera. Reluctantly letting him go, I moved back a bit, staring at his dishevelled hair. Damn, he looked so hot, even more so than before. And nope, it wasn't the sex hormones making me say that. There was something sinful, something even otherworldly about him, but I couldn't put my finger on what it was. He aimed his camera at me once again, and I felt so shy suddenly.

"Remember, I wanted to capture all the beauty Nature has to offer. And right now, the most beautiful creature is in front of me. May I?"

I nodded, totally flattered. Was he saying this to every girl? He snapped a few photos, then showed me the pictures. We laughed at some, then I blushed at others. His hands were all over me, caressing my back, playing with my hair, touching my bum. I couldn't keep my hands off him, either. Neither of us rushed to get dressed or swim to the shore. But there was only so long one could stand in the freezing water, especially if we weren't doing anything to warm us up. We turned our backs to the waterfall, and my heart broke a little. Was I going to see him again? I doubted that. The time to say goodbye was coming too fast, and I didn't like it. Not a tiny bit. I wanted to know so much about him, I wanted to tell him my life's story, but I walked silently beside him instead, holding hands. Oh, God, I realized I hadn't even told him my name yet. I cleared my throat, and we stopped in the velvety grass.

"Ruby. My name is Ruby."

Did I have to go James Bond on him? But he just nodded and smiled, squeezing my hand.

"I know. It's as beautiful as you are."

I didn't have much time to think about what he said, as he quickly added:

"We should repeat this, soon. The shooting, of course."

His grin said it all, as he brushed a curl of strawberry blonde hair off my shoulder, kissing the cane of my neck softly. I sighed, fighting back tears.

"Yeah, definitely. But how will we find each other?"

He smiled down at me, sapphire eyes twinkling in the sunlight.

"Just close your eyes, think about me, and I will be there."

I wanted to believe him, I really did. A normal guy would ask for my number, or my Facebook, or something. But then again, he was no ordinary guy, and that was why I had given in to temptation. I nodded, closing my eyes. I don't know what I expected, maybe that he would still be there when I opened them again. But alas, he was gone, and I was left alone to deal with my life. A previously unknown sadness darkened my heart, and it felt like I lost something I couldn't live without. Tears of anger, frustration, pain and love stained my cheeks, and I rushed back to get my rifle and make my way home.

~o~

By the time I put on my flip-flops, it was getting dark and I shivered in my summer dress. I looked around once more, trying to take in all the details, all the memories of our lovemaking, and that was when I spotted it. The camera was laying on the grass, its lens reflecting the disappearing light. I picked up the device, flicking through the pictures, and my heart clenched in my chest.

I had to try it, even if I felt insane. Kicking off my flip-flops I sat down onto the satin grass, looking around once more. A heavy sigh left my lips, and I closed my eyes. I pictured Eric's royal features, his charcoal hair, his sapphire eyes, the burgundy buttoned-down shirt, the silver-spotted black leather belt, the tight white pants, the black riding boots, everything, to the tiniest detail. I could almost smell his cologne, one I would recognize from a thousand others. I could almost feel his touch on my burning skin, his hands in my hair...

"Missed me already?"

My heart skipped a beat as I glanced up into a mocking pair of blue eyes. He held out a hand, and I took it gladly, letting him pick me off the ground. I wasn't sure whether I kissed him first, or if it was him, but the feeling was breath-taking nonetheless.

"You came back for me?"

I asked, with obvious hope in my voice. He raised a dark eyebrow, kissing me on the cheek.

"Nah, I just left my camera here."

I smacked him gently in the chest and he laughed, pulling me close.

"Of course I came back for you. I felt so silly leaving like this. Can you forgive me?"

It was my turn to mock him. Reaching for the hem of my 'I prefer animals to people' T-shirt, I pulled it over my head, then tossed the material onto the grass.

"Only if we get to do some more shooting."

And we did, for a few more hours. It worked. I thought about him, and he came back. After that fateful day, I sent Carl packing, and he didn't mind. He was glad, actually. As it turned out, the guy was with me only out of a sense of duty. Oh, well, his loss. I got to keep the cabin in the woods, and he got to keep his finger-licking habit. Finally, it was a win-win.

Eric became my anchor, whenever I wanted to disappear from the world, I just went back to the waterfall, closed my eyes, thought about him, and whispered his name and he came. It was truly magical. Was it real? I would say it doesn't really matter. Because, to me, this was the most real experience I have ever had. But I might tell you the secret one day. I might explain who (or rather what) Eric was. But for now, I'm just going to enjoy every single minute of it. And sometimes that's all we really need. No questions asked, just pure enjoyment. I hope all of you will find your Eric one day. I know I'm glad *I* did.

Love,

Ruby

~o~

HOW ABOUT THE ROOFTOP?

~o~

Hey, watch out!"
Too late.
I scowl, smoothing down my now coffee-stained T-shirt, trying to hold on to the little dignity I have left. I look up to see who my assailant is. Of course, today of all days I had to bump into a stranger who would pour steaming brown liquid all over my bruised ego. When was my life going to stop being a total mess?

I am momentarily distracted by the bluest eyes I've ever seen, but it doesn't last long. He is a man, and therefore he can be nothing else, but a total ass. My brown eyes shoot poisonous daggers his way, hoping they kill him on the spot. Well, they don't, they just make him smirk, while he looks me up and down, making my blood boil. But before I could say something snarky, he takes a step closer, fingering the spaghetti strap of my white (slash coffee-coloured) T-shirt.

"Well, well, I did warn you. But you know, you could always take this off."

I gasp, raising a hand, before I could even think about what I am doing. How dare he? But of course, he catches my wrist, and it never connects with his handsome face. Yeah, right, this guy might be God's gift when you look at him, but when he talks he confirms what I thought: he is an egoistic jerk, just like the rest of them. I glance around quickly, scanning the room, in case anyone saw what happened. But luck is on my side, at least in this tiny instance. Everyone is busy dancing with their partners, swaying to Brahms.

Typical.

I clear my throat, returning my gaze to the jackass, while smiling at him indignantly:

"I could, couldn't I? I guess that's the only thing guys like you can think of, right?"

Catherine – asshole 1:0.

I take a mental note to tap myself on the shoulder when I get home. Maybe I will even eat a box of chocolates, or some ice-cream. Oh, yes, I can do that now. I can do anything. And that includes slapping any guy who plays the jackass card on me. Who am I, some kind of a trophy? I realize too late that the annoying guy is still holding my right hand in his iron grip. He pulls me a tad bit closer, and I'm forced to look into those piercing blue eyes again.

There is a storm raging behind them, and I'm not sure if I'm more pissed off now or he is. God, I don't even know this asshole, and he managed to make all the nasty memories of last night come back in an instant. Will this ever stop?

He leans in towards my left ear, and a shiver runs through me, despite the heat and the steaming coffee still burning my stomach. And not from the right side, either, being stuck on my shirt and all.

"Guys like me, huh? You clearly have no idea what you are talking about. Well, I'm more than happy to show you…"

He lets go of my hand, running his fingers up my arms, awaking goose bumps on their way. But I ignore the electric shocks that try to grab my attention, and focus on my anger instead. This can only be happening to me, especially today. I must have it written all over my forehead: assholes hurry, here is a girl who just got dumped at the altar. Yeah, well, not exactly at the altar, but what difference does that make?

I push against the guy's chest, trying to stifle back my tears. Somehow I lost my will to come back with a witty response, so I just whisper before turning on my heels:

"You know what? I couldn't care less. You are all the same."

And with that I leave him near the canteen, mouth agape. That served him right. I don't need this right now. I don't need anyone to tell me how to behave, nor do I need to be seduced out of pity. I now have a massive coffee stain on my white T-shirt, so what? Worse things have happened, and I'm not looking for anyone's sympathy. Especially not a man's, whose first words when he meets a new girl are an attempt to get into her knickers.

Not me, mister.

Besides, I'm not here to get laid. God, I'm not even sure why I'm here anymore. This whole dance thing seemed like a brilliant idea. Well, when I was preparing for my wedding with Dom, that is. The so-called wedding was supposed to be four weeks from now, so it was the sensible thing to do that time. And now I'm here all alone, watching as four couples dance to Michael Bubble's *Sway*. My fiancé (or shall I say, ex-fiancé?) decided last night that the sensible idea for him was to say goodbye to our picket fence – and most importantly, me.

~o~

I swallow hard, wiping away a tear from the corner of my eyes. I keep reminding myself that he isn't worth it, that none of them are worth it, when there is a gentle tap on my shoulder and I jump, ready to fight whoever dared disturb my misery. I let out an exasperated sigh when I realize that it's Mr Idiot with those sizzling blue eyes.

He is smirking at my panicked face, but I guess I shouldn't have expected any less. He is a man, after all. I shake my head, bumping my fist "accidentally" into his stomach. Of course, my knuckles bounce off his six-pack, and that causes his mood to brighten even further. I curse silently, while Michael Bublé sings seductively in the background. Gosh, why can't I meet a guy like the singer? I bet *he* wouldn't dump anyone at the altar.

I hear my name from behind me, and I curse silently, ignoring the fact that this was at least the hundredth time I jumped (or cursed) today. Elise, our instructor is eyeing me suspiciously. I hold my breath, hoping she doesn't see the stain on my shirt, or the stain on my heart. But I'm not that lucky. Her sand-coloured eyes sadden, and she turns to the jackass, who's standing next to me now – too close for my liking, just for the record.

"Dominic, would you be so kind and lead this young lady to the dancefloor?"

"What?!"

We gasp in unison, and Elise looks startled for a second. Doesn't she realize that he isn't my fiancé? Can't she tell that I loath this guy, even though I have never met him before? Doesn't she know that I hate just about every guy on this planet right now? But then, just as quickly as her confusion arrived, it's gone, and she winks at me, a mischievous smile playing on her lips.

"Darling, dancing is the key to everything."

And with that she turns around and addresses the couples on the dancefloor. I tune out that moment, thinking about what she just said. How could dancing solve my problem? And why didn't she say anything? Except, she said way too much. Did Dominic tell her what had happened?

Dominic...

My eyes go wide, as realization dawns.

"Did she just say your name was Dominic?"

I think I spat the word out as if it was poisonous, but he doesn't even flinch. Nor does he answer my question. He grabs my hand instead, despite my obvious objection, and pulls me towards the other couples.

"What the hell are you doing? Let me go! Now!"

I basically scream, digging my heel in, but no use. Before I know it I'm in his arms, and we are swaying to the music. God, is this awful song on a loop? Okay, there is nothing wrong with the music, just with my company. His voice breaks through the mist that's beginning to cover my brain:

"It's easier if you relax and just go with the flow, you know."

What?

A minute ago he burnt me with coffee, and his words still sting. How could I relax?

"Look, I have no idea what game you are trying to play here, but it's not gonna work. Not now, not ever."

He pulls me close, swirling me towards the middle of the crowd. I involuntarily grab his shoulder, desperately holding on, inhaling his scent. Why does he have to smell so damn good? I groan, suddenly angrier at myself than him. His answer surprises me.

"I know. And I'm not trying anything, trust me."

His voice is apologetic, even a bit remorseful. I glance up, and his blue eyes smile at me. My heartbeat quickens and I ignore the pulsating sensation that all of this evokes down below. I'm not allowed to enjoy this. Not now, not with this guy. He doesn't only share a first name with my ex, but his arrogant attitude, too.

"That's it, ladies and gentlemen, just let the music lead the way…"

Elise's voice is dreamy, and I begin to wonder why she became a dance instructor. And more importantly, where does she get all this nonsense from?

"She is right, you know."

Dominic's voice catches me off-guard and I stumble. Unluckily, he holds me tight, so all I achieve is end up clinging to his chest. He stops, with me in his arms, his aqua eyes searching my chocolate pair.

"Are you alright?"

There, the dreaded question. How could I have thought I could pull this off without *my* Dom? The growing pit in my stomach doesn't let me answer, I just shake my head suddenly.

I have no idea why, but all it took was to share a dance with this stranger. Or maybe it was the seductive song, I wouldn't be able to tell. But before I know it I'm on tiptoe, reaching up to his face. He isn't taken by surprise, nor does he pull away. On the contrary, this Dominic knows exactly what I need. A little distraction. When my lips brush over his timidly, all the built-up tension from last night dissipates. All my worries, all my frustration is poured into one single kiss.

His hands are roaming on my back, caressing my bare skin above the white T, occasionally slipping under the spaghetti straps. The music stops, or it might as well be that the whole world ceases to exist. Maybe *I* ceased to exist last night when the other Dom uttered those hateful words. And now, I am coming back to life, full-swing. It might be my emotional roller-coaster ride, or the intoxicating song, but I feel light-headed and spent all of a sudden.

I break away, putting a few inches between our heaving chests. He leans close, placing a soft kiss on my forehead, then rests his against mine. We stand like that for a moment, while I try to figure out what just happened. What the hell got into me? Didn't I say that he was a jerk, and that this wasn't going to happen? I'm such a hypocrite. Maybe if I just explain to him what I'm going through...

"Look, Dominic, I'm so sorry..."

But he cuts me off, placing his fingers on my trembling lips. I glance up into his smouldering eyes, and for the first time I really appreciate the fact that I'm not alone right now. How could I have been such a jerk myself? I know I'm vulnerable to say the least, but I also can't help but notice his gorgeous features. The messy dark-brown hair that surrounds his face, the dark stubble, the inquisitive eyes, those kissable lips...

No, I'm not doing this again.

But before I know it, I lean in for another earth-shattering, soul-breaking kiss. He tastes and smells like pine trees, the forest, and the crisp midnight air. He tastes like freedom. His teeth graze my lower lip for a tiny second, but it's enough to make me want to get out of here with him – quickly. But of course I don't say a word. He doesn't need to know the effect he is having on me. The fact that he shares my ex's name pops into my mind, and all that 'once bitten, twice shy' crap.

It's him who pulls away though this time, leaving us both panting heavily. The dancefloor feels too crowded for my liking, and we bump into a couple. I glance their way, my heart clenching at the view. They seem to be so happy. Will they stay that way, or is he going to bail on her right before their wedding, too? Dominic's smooth voice brings me back to reality, caressing my senses:

"I'm not."

Huh? His words make no sense whatsoever. I raise an eyebrow, forgetting my predicament for a second. His stormy eyes bore into me, and I know there is no way out of this. I have to finish what I started. It's going to be the perfect rebound. No strings attached, no complicated relationship. No more heartbreak, no one to leave me stranded. Because this time I will be the one to say goodbye the morning after. I stir as Dominic's hand travels down my bare arm, and I close my eyes, contemplating my options. He must assume that I'm mad or deaf or something even worse, as he repeats what he said, grabbing my arm a bit too tightly, forcing me to open my eyes again.

"I said, I'm not sorry that you kissed me. On the contrary."

His smirk says it all, but I refuse to let it get to me this time. He is an asshole, but I don't care. At least he won't want to stick around and buy me dinner later. This, I can deal with. The other version, not so much. Once was more than enough. I tilt my head to the side, swaying my hips just a tiny bit. Michael Bublé starts to rhyme about the woman he hasn't met yet and I supress a chuckle. To think that I once wanted to dance to this at my wedding.

Oh, well, at least now I won't have to embarrass myself.

I decide that enough is enough. The lust in Dominic's eyes is palpable, and I'm not in the mood to deny my own pleasure. I have been doing that for long enough. For one night, I will be all he wants, and he will be mine. No questions asked. No rules. Just this stranger and me. I fumble around in my toasted brain for a place to drag his sexy butt, but he is faster. He raises an eyebrow, obviously figuring out what I'm thinking.

Does he do this often?

"How about the rooftop?"

I nod weakly, knees trembling and all.

Might as well be hanged for a sheep as for a lamb.

"Let's go."

He adds, leading the way already. I literally have to run to keep up with him. We rush past Elise, and a few things happen. Dominic smirks at her, she raises an eyebrow and I blush. I glance back over my shoulder mouthing 'sorry' at her, but she waves her hand, dismissing me and turning back to her other students. Not sure I should be offended or relieved, but I don't have time to think about her now anyway.

~o~

t so happens that the dance classes are in the middle of nowhere, in an abandoned warehouse. These places would normally freak me out, but this time it's different. Dominic leads me up a flight of stairs, and I can't help but wonder once again whether he does this often. Maybe that's why Elise waved at me, knowing what we were up to? I shudder, looking at the way his muscles flex under his black shirt. Oh, boy, I am in big trouble. His pine-tree scent fills my nostrils and I inhale sharply, bumping into his massive body. Apparently we reached the top.

The evening chill is settling in, making me shiver. But I don't care. Sheer anticipation rushes through every fibre of my body. I don't give a damn, whether he has done this a thousand times or not. Tonight he is doing it with me, and he is going to supply just the right amount of distraction I need.

Dominic turns to face me, his eyes searching mine. I only hesitate for a second, then kick the door shut behind us, leaving us stranded on the roof. Only him and me, and our sizzling desire. And yet, neither of us makes a move. I guess I should say something to break the spell, but we just stare at each other, making love with our eyes only.

Okay, enough is enough.

I reach out, popping the top button on his shirt clumsily. But he doesn't laugh. He just looks at my lips intently, his tousled hair falling into those gorgeous eyes. I gulp, popping another button, revealing more of his muscular chest. Then, led by a primal desire, I pull on the delicate material, and more buttons fall on the concrete floor. It feels silky under my touch, and the sensation is so erotic, it makes me moan. His eyebrows lift up as I glance at his six-pack. What is he, a bodybuilder?

"I haven't even touched you yet, girl. Who would have thought that you were so easy to please?"

My eyes flash, and my peach-coloured lips curl up into a wicked smile.

"Don't bet on it, smartass."

I trace his nipples with both hands, until the moment he grabs my wrists and holds my hands away from him. Oh, God, this is hot.

"Is that so?"

He tries not to laugh, and I find it hard to contain myself, too. Didn't think this would be so much fun. He lets go of my hands, and I nearly object, but then the incredible happens. My white slash coffee-coloured T-shirt ends up on the floor. How the hell did that happen? But I don't care, as the next minute my lips are on his neck, nibbling ferociously, as if this was the only thing I ever wanted.

He growls, and before I know it, he has me pinned up against the fire-exit's door. The tables have turned, and now he is biting down on my neck, making me lose my sense of time and reality. His left hand keeps my wrists pinned above my head, while his right one squeezes my boobs through the fabric of my bra. He pinches a sensitive and erect nipple, and I let out another moan. His head jerks up, my eyes gazing into the stormy sea.

"I don't think my task will be that *hard*."

He deliberately emphasizes the last word, and I involuntarily glance down, just before he presses his taught body against my soft flesh. I nod, knowing there is no point in denying what I feel anymore.

"I want you. I want you bad."

I say, just to make it easier, suddenly beginning to feel fed up with the sexy banter. Enough talk already, where is the action? That's why we are up here, right?

"Not so fast."

He says, and swiftly turns me around. I'm facing the door now, my head spinning. The evening breeze picks up my skirt, but it might as well be his hands, especially because a minute later the material ends up on the floor, too. Not that I mind, not at all. Dom pulls my white lace panties aside, humming in appreciation. I think I blush, but once again, he doesn't leave me too much time to nurse my doubts, as his tongue darts out, exploring my folds. I close my eyes, enjoying the way his lips drive me crazy.

His stubble tickles my sensitive skin, and his rough fingers knead my butt cheeks. I push back against his lips, and he lets out a chuckle, pulling away. I groan, letting him know that I'm not one he can boss around. I am normally the one who takes the lead.

"Not tonight, Catherine. Just let it go."

Catherine? How does he know my name? But before I could ask, his tongue connects with my clit, sending my heart on another spin. His tongue flickers over the sensitive spot, and I can already feel my insides quiver, when he pushes a finger inside. Only till the first knuckle, just to tease me. Then he pulls it out, his tongue leaving my clit at the same time.

"Let go."

He repeats, but I'm stubborn. I shake my head, sending my chocolate curls flying around my shoulders. He breaths against my pussy lips, but refuses to touch me this time. I choose this time to voice my question, probably flattening the mood straight away.

"How do you know my name?"

He snickers, nibbling on the back of my right thigh, making me shudder. His thumb brushes past my clit, obviously in an attempt to distract me from my mission. I clench my thighs together, which makes him laugh whole-heartedly. The sound goes to my head instantly (and to other parts of my body, too).

"Elise shouted it over the dance floor, remember? I'm pretty sure the whole group knows who the only single woman was there tonight."

That's it. I snap.

"Don't you dare think you know everything about me! You don't! I'm not..."

But I'm unable to finish. I try to turn around and push him away, but he straightens his back, and envelopes me in his arms, pulling me close to his heart.

"Catherine, I'm so sorry. I didn't mean to... I'm sorry."

My resistance fades and I'm just standing there, half-naked on the rooftop, with a stranger, who just insulted me. But is it his fault? As I remain silent, he adds, genuinely worried this time:

"Look, he didn't deserve you. He is an idiot, if he doesn't see what he is missing right now."

His hold loosens and I turn around, looking into his aqua eyes. I lift up my chin defiantly, refusing to weep.

"I don't need your pity. I don't want you to fuck me just because you feel sorry for me."

There. As soon as I say those words, the levy breaks and I fall into his arms, now voluntarily. He wraps his arms around me protectively, promising never to let me go. And that's all I need for now. I inhale his heavenly scent, wanting to experience the freedom I felt earlier.

"Hush now, it's going to be okay."

He caresses my hair gently, and I stifle a sob. I feel awful all of a sudden. I'm pretty sure he doesn't need this right now. He brought me up here for a quicky, and he ended up playing nurse. I push away, looking up into his gorgeous eyes. There is no sign of pity in them, no. He wants me, and not because I was left a month before my impending nuptials. He wants me for *me*. That surely counts for something? A small smile tugs at my lips, and I suddenly feel the freedom again.

"What's so funny?"

He eyes me suspiciously, probably wondering whether I'm going mad.

Well, welcome to the club.

I place my hand on his face, enjoying the way his stubble insults my palm, and all my senses.

"Nothing, just... I'm just glad you are here, that's all."

Which is probably the dumbest thing to say, but hey? What do I know? I haven't dated for ages. But it seems to have worked, as Dominic smiles, cupping my hand in his. His eyes turn a shade darker, and his gaze travels down my body.

Guess that's my cue.

I glance at his bulging pants, but before I could do anything, he shakes his head, a wicked smile spreading on his lips.

"Oh, no, you won't. What did I ask you?"

He is mocking me now, and I bite my lower lip, rolling my eyes. His left eyebrow shoots up, and I give in.

"Okay, fine, I will let go."

Another eyebrow goes up, and I snicker.

"I'm sorry, I didn't quite catch that?"

I smack him in the chest, regretting it in an instant, as he grabs my hand once more. I try to raise on my tiptoe and kiss him, but he is holding me firmly.

Jeez.

"Very funny. Okay, you won. You are the boss. But only for tonight."

His aqua eyes lit up with blue fire as he turns me around, pushing me on the cold concrete roof.

"Oh, babes, one night won't be enough. Not even close."

I gasp, not wanting to notice the suggestion behind his words.

Oh, why can't this be simple?

~o~

He grabs my hips, pulling my backside against his shaft, and I forget that I didn't want a relationship. I forget that I hate every single man on earth. Gosh, I even forget what the other Dominic looks like. I let out a moan as he pushes my panties aside again, his rough hands connecting with my sensitive skin. He smacks my bottom, then he smacks it again. It feels so good that I don't want him to stop. I have no idea when he removed his pants, but the next time his hand comes down on my left cheek, his cock slides into my dripping pussy.

"Oh, God..."

I can hear him smirk behind me, and he says between two earth-shattering thrusts:

"You can call me Dom, you know."

What a jerk.

But before I could even think of a witty comeback he has me trembling. I'm on all fours, being fucked by a stranger, on the roof of an abandoned warehouse, a few hours after my fiancé bailed on me.

Go figure.

And yet (or maybe because of all of this), I don't hold back anymore. I push back against Dominic's dick, with as much force I can muster. I'm not sure anymore whether he is fucking me, or if it's the other way around. Not that I care. Not as long as he gives me what I need.

"Let it go."

Just like a broken record. Except this time I listen. And obey. His words are my undoing, and I cum with such a force I fear it will send us both off the roof. Even if we are miles away from the edge. My whole body is pulsating around him, and it feels like I never knew what a real orgasm felt like. I'm serious, I can see stars, the moon, the whole works.

"Oh fuck!"

Yeah, that was me, too. As he thrusts deeper, I lose control. Exactly the way he wanted. I grind my hips against his, and his cock is balls-deep inside me. The feeling is bold, yet exquisite. He reaches below my belly, and his thumb presses down on my clit, while he pounds me from behind. I feel like my insides are on fire, yet the cool breeze makes me shiver. I chuckle, suddenly remembering Katy Perry's song, 'Hot & Cold'. Although I'm sure she had something else in mind when she wrote it. Not to mention that she is left at the altar, too. Well, at least in the song. Dominic pulls out, bringing me back to reality and I voice my disappointment this time.

"Why did you stop?"

He presses the tip of his cock against my clit, and I close my eyes.

"I'm in control, remember?"

I nod, unable to say a word. Right now I don't care about my dignity, nor what he will think of me later. Right now I just want him to fuck me. I think he realizes that I'm not one to mess with, especially tonight, because he plunges back in, making me jerk forward in pure ecstasy.

"Say my name, Catherine. Say it."

I gasp and even wiggle a bit, his words like a stab wound in my heart.

No, I can't...

He grabs my hair, leaning close to my ear. The motion of his hips is steady, and I know I'm close again.

"Please, don't make me..."

He stops, and that's when the first tear rolls down my cheek. Then he starts moving slowly, taking me by surprise. I scream, shuddering all over.

"Dominic... I want you to fuck me."

The words are out before I know what I'm saying. His pace quickens, and I wait for the pang of guilt, the pain, the misery. But all I can feel is pleasure. I don't understand it at first, I just close my eyes, enjoying the blissful moment. His cock swells inside me, and he groans loudly, finally exploding. I ride out his orgasm with him, in a daze. The cold suddenly reaches me, and my nipples harden under the fabric of my bra.

He pulls me up, smoothing my hair down, and I smile. He clears his throat, obviously searching for the right words. I'm faster this time.

"You don't have to say anything, I get it."

He eyes me suspiciously, raising a dark eyebrow:

"You do?"

I nod, brushing away a stray strand of hair from his gorgeous face.

"Yes, I finally get it. I needed this. All of it."

Including saying his name, but he doesn't need to know that. Somehow, by associating it with something good, after all the bad, I let it all go. It might have been only a few hours ago that the other Dominic dumped me, but I guess I gave up on him long before that. He was just not worth it. Aqua eyes burn into my chocolate brown and I gulp as he leans in for a lingering kiss. What was it about one night not being enough? When he finally pulls away, his eyes are beaming with myriads of emotions.

"So did I, Catherine, so did I."

Now it's my turn to look at him questioningly, and he lets out a frustrated sigh.

"Look, I didn't want to tell you this, but I guess it doesn't matter now anyway."

He is searching my face for encouragement, and I nod, not wanting to interrupt him. Wherever this is going, I'm dying to find out.

"I saw you here the other day. With him. In fact, I've been here all along. You didn't see me, because you were so engrossed with your fiancé, but I saw you alright. And you know what?"

"What?"

I exhale sharply, my voice a tiny whisper.

"I could tell even back then that you weren't happy. You only had eyes for him, yes, but it was rather a case of obligation. The way you looked at me tonight, well, let's just say you never looked at him that way."

I raise an eyebrow, folding my arms in front of my chest. His eyes follow the motion and I chuckle.

"Is that so? Well, don't let it get to your head though. Otherwise there won't be any space for me, because your ego will push me out."

He pulls me close, and I'm not laughing anymore. Boy, I'm not even breathing.

"No chance, Catherine. Absolutely..."

A slight kiss on my lips.

"No..."

Another feather-light caress.

"Chance."

I sigh as he nibbles on my neck. To hell with my promise. To hell with everything. If I will ever get burnt again, this guy will totally be worth it. He finishes his task, leaving a red mark I'm sure.

"Okay, Mr Jerk, what do you say we head inside? We might catch the end of the class."

He smirks at me, and nods, handing me my skirt. Except he pulls it away the last minute, throwing it back on the floor, a wicked glint in his eyes.

Oh, well, I never really liked that song anyway...

~o~

CONJURED LOVER

~o~

Okay, so the only thing I'm missing is sage. Out of all things, it's fricking sage."

I let out a frustrated sigh, especially because I know that I had it on my list. I had it on *both* lists, to be precise. Yes, I will need to go to the shop again, because I will need the nasty spice for cooking, too. *Tomorrow*. Or the day after. But tonight, I need to focus. I glance to my right, watching in awe as Snowball lives up to his name, curling up in front of the fireplace.

Oh, how much I wish I was a cat right now.

But then again, I know I must be careful what I wish for. Especially since I 'realized' that my mother was a Wicca. Cool, right? Well, not so much if she leaves you when you are only three, and you are forced to learn everything for yourself (and by yourself). And that includes cooking, boys, and now magic.

And my father? Well, he is great, thank you very much. Or I guess he is, somewhere in the Alps, having fun with his girlfriend and her kids. The kids he is raising as his own, by the way. But it's okay. I can cope with it, I really can. All of it. Well, apart from the magic part, if I'm honest.

Let me get one thing straight: I don't want this. I have never had any intentions of stepping into *her* footsteps. Not even for a minute. I wanted to find my own path, I wanted to be different. Yet here I am, being so desperate that I'm casting a spell. And a love spell at that. Funny, right?

Okay, I'm not laughing. I'm thinking of doing everything else *but* laugh. Like run out of the house or sink below the floorboards. Or just simply run, and never look back. Start over somewhere, where nobody knows me. Sure thing. Although that might be an option even here, because I've never made any friends. Not real ones anyway. Having to grow up when you are basically still a child does that to you. Go figure.

So, yes, no luck in the guys' department, either. I didn't have a mother to tell me about my period, let alone sex, nor did I have a father to warn me about the dangers of letting a guy walk me home. Until that 'special' school education, I thought that storks brought babies and dropped the cute little things onto your doormat.

Uh-huh, I wasn't the sharpest tool in the shed.

And I can't exactly say that I know too much about sex now, either, even at the age of twenty-five. All my so-called friends have had five-six (or some of them even dozens) of boyfriends, and I only had two. Not to mention that they sucked. One of them quite literally, deciding that he preferred boys. Not the best way to gain some confidence, especially since he broke up with me two weeks before discovering his true 'calling'. But what about my own identity, my own calling? I always knew I was different, weird even. But how could I know who I truly am, when my whole life is based on lies?

Snowball reminds me that I have an important task, meowing eagerly. Yep, he can truly sense when I'm in a bad mood, and this is one of those times. Probably not the best time to cast a love spell, but I don't have another chance. Not for a long time. Oh, I did my research. And I was thorough, like always. I need a full moon, and this one is an extra special one, because it falls on All Hallows' Eve. Witches (or Wicca, as I understand they call themselves nowadays) believe that the veil between our world and that of the spirits is the thinnest this time of the year. Anything can come through, not just messages.

But it works both ways, so we can send a message to the Universe, too, and it's extremely likely that it will be answered. I guess you can imagine my initial reaction. Yep, wanted to stick three fingers in the air, hoping the Universe could read between the lines. But then I thought better of it.

You probably think I should be asking for the whereabouts of my mother or my father, but I simply don't care. I haven't seen them (or heard from them) in exactly 22 years, and I've been fine, I really have been. Not gonna start to be a cry-baby tonight, that's for sure. So, back to the spell. Witches say this time is perfect, and it only happens every few years. Well, being single for the past four, I would rather not wait any longer, if it's up to me. And, as it turns out, it *is* probably up to me.

Oh, that bloody sage.

Why don't they attach an emergency guide in case you don't have all the ingredients? I can't believe that every single witch goes to the shop, remembering everything, every single time they want to cast their spell. Surely, they must have a substitute for these herbs. You know what? I don't care. I don't even believe in this stupid thing.

Why am I doing it then?!

Emily, focus. That's it. Now, where was my pen? Ah, behind the candle. Okay, I will do this, sage or no sage.

Lighting the candle is easy, as is anointing it with the required oils. They actually smell really nice. They remind me of *her*. Well, what I can remember, that is. I could never place the smell, but now at least I know. With a bitter smile I note the faint scent of sage, which might be an ingredient of one of the oils. Great, that will do. As soon as I smear the last drops onto the side of the pink candle, it sizzles a bit. Trying to calm my breath, I reach for the piece of paper, then start writing.

Gentle. Caring. Affectionate. Attentive.

Snowball meows again and I scrap the paper, tossing it in the already overflowing bin. Why is it so hard to come up with the characteristics I'm looking for in a man? Why can't I know what (or who) I'm craving for, just like Christine or Hannah? They are always so sure, and then of course they end up with the guy of their dreams.

And me?

I might have my ideal guy in mind, but somehow, I always choose the safe option. Aka the guy that I don't even find attractive. As long as they like me, I think that's enough for both of us. Well, clearly, if that was the case, I wouldn't be trying to summon my dream guy, would I? Or conjure, or whatever the spell said. It isn't going to happen anyway.

Maybe I'm just trying to prove to myself that this shit doesn't work, and that my mother left me for nothing. I mean, how could magic be so important that she leaves her own daughter for it, driving her husband insane at the same time, so he is forced to do the same?

Okay, back to the so-called spell. Taking a deep breath, I close my eyes, trying to imagine how the man of my dreams would look like. If this won't work, I might as well go for the real thing, right? Where's the harm? It takes a few minutes to form a mental image, but I'm getting there. He disappears a few times, moves in and out of focus, until I can concentrate enough to maintain the picture.

I nod to myself, then open my eyes again, trying to capture everything I saw. No, he wasn't gentle or caring. He was hot, sinful, and dominating. He took what he wanted – what *I* wanted as well. He loved me with such a passion that made my head spin and consumed my heart and soul. He was dangerous, the kind that burns you out in a second, if you aren't careful. And to hell with being careful when he holds you in his arms.

He is the type that melts your heart (and panties), just by looking at you with those smouldering eyes. Yes, I think that kind of passion is exactly what I need right now. Maybe that's what I have always needed, even if I didn't know I wanted it. I might have lived a sheltered life to date, and it was safe, I will give myself that. But it was as boring as it could ever get, with no risks involved. Well, no risks of losing someone again. My heart never got involved, so I wouldn't have to go through that excruciating pain ever again.

Snowball scratches the leg of my chair, stirring me back to reality. This is so silly, me crying about my past all over again, when I promised I wouldn't do it anymore. With a sigh I fold the piece of paper, finally happy with the outcome. Okay, I have the list, what's next? Oh, I have to burn it in the pink candle's flame, then bury the ashes in my front garden. There is just one problem with that: I don't *own* a front garden. Again, a small cactus pot will have to do. I think I will place it on the windowsill, so the full moon can shine on it. Even the thought makes me shiver.

Careful not to burn my loft apartment down, I throw the folded paper into the tiny flames. It might just be the strangeness of tonight, but for a second I could swear I see the flames take on a neon green hue, but then it's gone, and so is the piece of paper. Wow, that was cool, and faster than I imagined.

All I have to do now is bury the ashes and wait. With trembling hands, I reach for the tiny cactus, silently thanking it for its service all these years. Who knows what will happen to the poor thing now, that I'm using it as a carrier for my spell? I just hope it won't turn into the man, because then I'm screwed. The idea makes me chuckle, and, for the first time in a long time, I feel like I'm ready for whatever comes next.

Boy, am I wrong...

~o~

Patting the smooth soil down I sigh heavily, already knowing just what a fool I am. Yeah, sure, the guy I secretly dream about, the one I haven't even met yet, is going to appear in my life miraculously. Just because I cast a spell. Just because so-called magic is in my blood. Please, give me a break. I feel a sudden urge to put the candle out and go to bed, but as I reach for the flame, it flickers again, as if trying to escape my murderous touch. The idea alone is ridiculous, and if I wasn't so pissed off right now, I would probably laugh at my stupidity.

Okay, I can do this.

Taking a deep breath, I brace myself to blow out the mesmerizing flame, when the clock strikes midnight and I jump out of my skin. Goosebumps are fighting for a space on my arms, but there isn't much left to spare, considering that I'm scared shitless. Something has changed, and I can feel it. The clock strikes again, and a shiver runs through me. It's as if I wasn't alone in the room. The air becomes chilly, and Snowball gives a low growl, then a hissing sound, just before disappearing behind the sofa. I can't blame him, because I wish I could do the same.

But I'm paralyzed. I gulp, unable to take my eyes off the now pinkish-orange flames. They seem to change colour by the second, flickering, sizzling, playfully tangling my nerves into a thousand knots. Their dance is so beautiful, magical even, and I'm under their spell. For a brief moment I wonder what's going on, but then the clock's chime rings in my ears once more, and the now emerald flames flicker again, leaving me breathless and empty.

The void that has always been in my soul, only hidden in the deepest corners is now more painful than ever, and I'm afraid it will consume me. I close my eyes, letting the void take over. I can't breathe, I can't say anything, just sit there, with my eyes closed and my heart wide open. Whatever is in the room, whatever is here to take me, I'm ready.

Waiting for the inevitable, I hum a song I still remember from my childhood. There is a faint touch on my shoulder, a tender caress, and the goose bumps come to life once more, demanding attention. The motion sends shivers down my spine, through my soul, my entire being. It's both a delicious and scary experience, but one that I want very much. So much so, that it forces me to open my eyes and glance back over my shoulder. Except, nothing could have prepared me for the transformation that happens in front of my eyes.

I gasp, and might even have screamed a little, if I didn't lose my will to speak. I get up and walk up to the mirror. One step at a time.

That's it, Emily, you can do this.

I stop in front of the mirage, unable to believe my eyes, but also incapable of taking my eyes off it, in case it disappears. The scene is so clear, so real, I feel like I only need to reach out and touch it, to be a part of it all. The full-length mirror that used to be home to all my insecurities, all my teenager anger, fear, frustration, and sadness, now depicts a totally different picture.

It's still my reflection, but somehow I don't recognize the woman staring back at me. Her face is flushed, her freckles have disappeared, and her previously fox-coloured hair is now a healthy (and quite seductive) shade of auburn. And her eyes speak volumes of the storm that's raging inside her fragile soul. Except, I don't feel fragile anymore. Gazing into the mirror makes me feel sexy, desirable even. I don't know how, but all of a sudden I see just how strong I am, how I am whole already. And I have achieved that all on my own, without the help of anyone.

I involuntarily twirl a curl between my fingers, just to make sure I'm not dreaming. The mirror was showing the truth, I have changed. But didn't I cast a love spell? Could it work this way, too? To help me love myself? But then it still doesn't make sense, except... I reach out, placing my palms onto the mirror's surface and close my eyes for a second, wondering if the new me will disappear when I open them again.

But something else happens. Something much scarier. Something I can't explain. Something I don't want to explain. Instead of the cool, hard glass, my open palms touch something silky smooth, velvety, and oh-so-alive. Yes, I can hear someone's heartbeat in my mind, I can feel the pulsation under my fingertips.

My own heart speeds up to match the pace, and I'm too scared to open my eyes. A pair of strong hands slowly envelop mine, holding me still, before I could fall into nothingness.

Emily...

No, I don't want this, not yet.

Emily... Open your eyes...

No.

Trust me, you are safe. You wanted this, remember?

The voice is coming from deep inside my mind, and I might as well be losing my grip on reality for all I know. There is that gentle touch on my shoulder once more, followed by a featherlight kiss on my neck, and I let out a whimper. It is too good, too painful to be true. It speaks of love, happiness, and ecstasy. And yes, lots of pleasure.

And it could all be mine. It could be, but when? And how?

Just open your eyes...

I finally do as the voice says, and I swear I don't even gasp when his turquoise eyes search my face. Nor do I squirm when his hands leave mine and travel up my arms, resting at my shoulders. He probably just wants to steady me, but his touch is everything *but* soothing. His hair falls onto his muscular shoulders in waves, almost like a mirage that could disappear any second. The thought alone makes my stomach do a double-take. Whoever this guy is, I don't want him to go anywhere.

Then I won't.

I nod, as if him talking to me in my mind was the most natural thing on earth. Well, we might not even be on earth anymore, but I don't give a damn. I wanted to start anew somewhere else anyway, didn't I? As if on cue, a gentle breeze caresses my skin, bringing with it the scent of freedom and adventure. I take a deep breath, inhaling it all. As I'm about to take in my beautiful stranger, he lets go of my arms and takes a step back.

No, please don't go.

I thought I was shouting, but my voice was only in my head, as it seems. And yet, a cheeky smile appears on those kissable lips, softening his masculine features.

Just thought I would give you the option to have a proper look.

I must admit, I appreciate the idea. The way he is standing in the middle of the field now, surrounded by nothing but the vast array of greens of all hues, with his devilishly handsome features, he makes the perfect contrast. I don't even care why he is dressed in a white shirt, brown pants and a pair of black riding boots, nor do I want to notice the sword by his side, or the bow hung over his back. He isn't dangerous, or at least not in that way. He wouldn't hurt me. After all, I conjured him.

No, you didn't.

I raise an eyebrow at that, and he finally speaks. I mean for real this time, and not only in my head. God, his voice could be used to move mountains.

"Although I must admit, your power surprised me. You weren't supposed to be able to do that."

"What is it exactly that I did?"

Good, I found my own voice. Hopefully I'm not going crazy then. He motions behind my back, and I turn around, maybe too quickly. He steadies me again, this time pulling me close to his chest, and I swallow hard. Not just because his muscles are pressing into my back, but because of what's in front of me. My loft apartment, my cat curled up in front of the fireplace, and the candle on the small table. The only 'problem' is that I'm not there. I'm on the other side of the mirror, as strange as that sounds. I shake my head, and ask the only thing I can think of:

"How?"

He lets out a sigh behind me, and it makes me shiver. *Do I want to know?*

"Magic."

I turn around in his arms, realizing a moment too late that it was a bad idea. His eyes seem to be glowing now, and the turquoise iris has a few spots of amethyst in it. Before I could say anything, he continues in his deep ocean voice:

"Although you didn't conjure me, you did open up the portal that led you to me, to my world. I didn't think it was possible, but I underestimated you. Will you forgive me, My Lady?"

I blink once, then I blink again, in complete shock. I glance back over my shoulder, afraid that the mirror would disappear, and I would have no way back. But then, would I miss anything, apart from Snowball? Turning back to him, it's my turn to search his handsome face, but the previous glow is gone. His eyes are turquoise again, and boy, do they make me hot and bothered.

"I have so many questions..."

He places a warning finger onto my lips, and I gulp.

"There will be plenty of time for that... Later. But tell me, did you really cast that spell to *talk* to me?"

And with that, his finger traces a lazy line along my lower lip, then my jaw, while the amethyst spots reappear in his eyes, along with the lust I was hoping for all along. It makes my head spin, but I would give anything just to look into them for all eternity. But I don't.

~o~

He is right. I'm not here to talk or simply look at him. I know that he is basically a stranger, and we are in a strange land (or I'm going crazy), but either way, I feel like I have known him longer than I've known myself. I seem to recall the snake tattoo on his left arm, or the way he likes his coffee. I seem to *remember* his touch, his kiss, the way his love tastes. I have no idea how this is possible, but right now I don't care.

With all the strength I can muster, and before I change my mind, I raise on tiptoe and plant a tentative kiss on his full lips, one that he returns eagerly, and with a tad bit more passion than I can take without losing my mind completely. And then it hits me. This happened before, with him, maybe in another lifetime. It was always meant to be. Opening up to him comes so naturally that it's almost scary. No, not almost. He must sense my hesitation, as he is the one who pulls away, keeping me at arms' length.

"Maybe we should stop."

He whispers between two ragged breaths, and I have to give him that, he is a gentleman. I frown, then remembering something, smile innocently.

"Maybe we should."

I can almost feel his pain at the rejection, but he nods, takes a step back, reaches for my hand, then lifting it up to his lips he places a soft kiss onto my palm. A kiss that's meant to be a sign of respect, but to me, it's much more. Pictures of a past I never knew I had come flooding to my mind, images of him and me, images of us. Some of them painful, others mildly erotic – and the rest, well... Not so mildly. I don't think he saw this one coming, but from his burning gaze I know he felt it, too. I nod, as if giving my approval to myself, then shoot him the most seductive smile I have up my sleeve.

"But then again, I don't think stopping was on my mind when I cast that spell, either."

I don't know who closes the distance between us. It doesn't even matter. What matters is that we both want to live and relive those memories of another lifetime, while creating some new ones to remember in the next. Time stops right here, right now, there is only this one moment we will always call our own, no matter what happens later. No matter what happens when I go back to the other side of the mirror, to my world. Now, right now, I'm in *his* world. And, as they say, when in Rome, do as the Romans do. Who am I to argue with that?

Suddenly his lips are on mine, and he kisses me as if this was what he has been waiting for all his life. And I kiss him back as if my life depended on it. It occurs to me, that up until this moment, I only existed, but I never lived. I never loved. Not with all my heart and soul, not pouring all of me into the notion. One single kiss is my undoing, and it threatens to spin me out of both his and my world. But isn't this what I wanted? Spell or no spell, he *is* everything I ever wanted.

Hell, he used to be mine.

Why haven't I found him in this life until now? He clears his throat and looks away, as if I said something awkward. Yeah, right, I will have to get used to this telepathic thingy...

"This is going to sound strange."

I raise an eyebrow at him, and he lets out a small chuckle. Oh, God, is he cute when he does that, or what?

"Okay, maybe not stranger than any of this. You know, even soulmates don't always spend all their life together. They don't even meet in every lifetime. Sometimes one of them isn't ready, the feelings they get when they are around each other become too strong to bear. But when they do meet and accept who they really are to each other, well... That's just epic."

There is a wicked grin on his gorgeous face now, and I can't help but grin back.

"And let me guess: you are about to prove your point, am I right?"

He nods again, and the amethyst sparkles return, taking my breath away.

"But first, I want to show you some *real* magic."

And with that, those amethyst spots grow larger, until they consume his entire iris. It is beautiful and mesmerizing. I feel like I am flying, and everything seems so small. I gasp when I realize what is happening. I look around, which only confirms what I feared. I'm floating mid-air, and he is holding me up with his gaze. Oh, wow, now it was me, who didn't see this one coming. Strangely enough, I'm not scared.

On the contrary. I make birdlike movements with my arms, pretending they are wings. His laughter is like music to my ears, and I think I fall in love with him a little more. After we had our fun, another type of fun begins, but we are no longer laughing. I end up on my back, and my clothes disappear. The velvety grass is tickling my back and bare bottom, but it's a delicious feeling. If anything, it adds to my arousal. Hmm, I'm beginning to like his world.

Well, actually...

"Real magic? Didn't you say that *I* had powers, too?"

He raises an eyebrow, now kneeling between my bare thighs. A shiver runs through me as I picture his face buried between them, but I must contain myself — for a little longer. Focusing all my energy and willpower, I concentrate on his shirt, and wait. And... Nothing happens. Except that I make him laugh. Which in turn makes me furious. What do they say about magic being intensified by strong emotions?

"Honey, it took me years to learn how to..."

He loses his train of thought when his shirt vanishes into thin air, followed by his pants, the sword and the bow. My head hurts a little, but it was totally worth it. And so was the admiration on his face. *Priceless*.

"You were saying?"

But he thinks better of underestimating me again. Instead, he continues what he started a moment ago. Trailing soft (and occasionally not-so-soft) kisses along my inner thigh, he inches up towards my pussy, and I can't wait for him to get there. But he doesn't, at least not before his tongue and fingertips travel down my other leg first.

He looks into my eyes, and those amethyst spots pull me in, while his tongue circles my clit. He gently bites down, and I can see the ghost of a smile on his lips before my back arches off the ground. The feeling is too much, he was right. But I wouldn't trade it for all the riches of the world. Both his, and mine.

He continues his sweet torture, kissing, sucking, biting. It feels like an eternity passes, and maybe it does. The first ripple of orgasm takes me by surprise, and I almost pass out from the sensation. But I don't, and he continues licking my pussy, torturing my clit, as if he didn't just witness my whole world crumble. Needless to say that I have no energy to argue, but a girl has to try, right?

"Mhm... no... em, yes... wait.. it's my... turn..."

Next time. Now I need you too bad.

I fleetingly note that we are back to that telepathic talk, but before I could think about something, he pushes his impressive (and quite obvious) erection into my slit, and all wittiness leaves my being. All I can do is hold on to his shoulders, digging my nails into his ripped flesh. He groans, but grabs hold of my hands, lifting them above my head. His amethyst spots grow once more, and I can feel something tighten around my wrists. I look up, only to see his belt keeping my hands locked above my head. Magic again, how very clever. His teeth graze the sensitive spot behind my ear, before he whispers:

"If you kept that up, I wouldn't last a minute."

And with that, he starts moving his hips, and I'm only too eager to match his thrusts. I now know that I could probably break free using my will. If I wanted to, that is. I know that my moans are getting louder, but I don't care. It isn't like anyone could hear us, and even if they could, they would be in for a treat. Hell, I know *I am*. It's as if we fit together perfectly, our motions are coordinated. Like those ballet dancers that practice for years.

Can we practice this for years?

His answer doesn't register, as it's swept away by another otherworldly orgasm that rocks my world. God, I feel like it even shook the ground. But yet again, I don't have time to come down from my natural high, because he lifts my legs up higher, while his hands move underneath my buttocks, thus elevating my hips. I've never tried this position before, but then again, I never had a proper lover before him, either.

Still, I can tell that he is near. I look at those amethyst-stained turquoise eyes a little longer, trying to drink it all in for later. The light brown hair that falls smoothly onto his shoulders, the muscles that move whenever he enters me or draws out. The myriads of emotions and memories that radiate from this eyes, the ones that are reflected in my green pair. All the things we used to tell each other, all the things I want to hear in this lifetime, too. I lost count of the times he took me to Heaven, both in previous lifetimes and in this one, but one thing is clear: I was right. I have never been loved before.

Not like this.

Coming back to Earth (or wherever we are) is a shocking and unwelcome feeling. I know that sooner or later I will have to go back through the looking glass. Funny, I don't remember Alice having such wonderful adventures. But then again, that story was for kids, right? I look around once more, so that I can always remember this place. Because, according to the Wicca, opportunities like this don't come often. I look into his now turquoise eyes, and I can tell he is thinking about the same thing. An idea starts to form in my head.

"Can I stay?"

My voice is shaky, almost childish, and his expression changes instantly. I don't like his look, not a single bit.

"Not yet."

The words are out before I could take them back, but the voice seems like someone else's:

"Can you come with me then?"

He shakes his head again, and my heart sinks. I nod between two sobs, turning towards the mirror. Its smoky interior, the small loft apartment that I once called my own, seem to be repelling me now. So strange that when I got here, I was afraid that I couldn't go back, and now that I am forced to, I'm scared I will never find my way back here. *Talking about never belonging anywhere.* Suddenly, I can feel his touch on my neck, a gentle caress. I look back behind my shoulder, and he kisses me gently. Saying goodbye. I break away a minute too early. I have never been good at this kind of thing.

I raise my hands, placing each palm onto the cold, hard surface of the mirror, then close my eyes and wait. I don't look back. I don't want him to see my tears, nor do I want to see him waving goodbye. I don't want to remember all that could have been mine. The now familiar dizziness takes over, and when I open my eyes, the levy breaks. I'm back in my loft, and Snowball stirs in his sleep, meowing, before turning his other side. I glance at the candle, just to catch the last flames burning down. With heart in my chest I turn around, touching the mirror. I don't even know his name, and he has disappeared for ever. Why did I have to come back? Why?

I want to be with you. Please, let me go back.

But nothing happens. Stupid mirror. I bump my fist into it, but all it gives me in return is my reflection. I have changed, I know that now. Nothing will ever be the same. But I notice something else as well, between two sobs. I wipe my eyes, looking at the small medallion. Its turquoise stone is glowing in the disappearing candlelight, and the flecks of amethyst cast mysterious shadows around the room.

You can come back, anytime you like. The medal will help you, my love.

I nod, my sobs slowly easing into a gentle laughter. I will go back through the mirror, many times. In fact, I feel like I belong there, with him. I belong there with you.

You do. I'm yours, and you are mine, for all eternity. Oh, and I'm Aiden, by the way.

Aiden, of course. No wonder I have always found that name sexy as hell. Okay, he is right. And yes, I have changed. But not enough, not yet. I need to know who I am, I need to know how is it possible that I can wield such powerful magic, without ever practicing. I need to find my mum and get some answers. I need to know the truth. And all of it this time. I walk up to the fireplace, gently caressing Snowball out of his slumber. He looks at me sleepily, and I whisper as I gaze into his emerald eyes:

"I hope you are ready for an adventure, little one."

~o~

A tempting taste of other, bite-size erotica, from the naughty pen of Timea Tokes:

~o~

THREE BILLIONAIRES & ME
(SAMPLE)

Yes?'

There is silence on the other end of the line, then, when I'm about to hang up, the rich guy with the smooth voice says, sounding clipped and professional:

'Good evening, Miss Nelson. If it works for you, I would like to use our first names for the night.'

I bite my lower lip, closing my eyes at the same time. I can't help but picture the guy this sexy voice belongs to. Part of me is even getting aroused by the prospect of being owned by him. Silly, right? I am proving to be the exact same as everyone else, and I'm not even as ashamed of it as I should be. Here I am, laying on a hotel bed naked, after auctioning myself off for one million pounds.

'Sure, Mr?'

I ask, purring. He lets out a sigh, and I can almost see him shake his head.

'Alec. My name is Alec. But please, Olivia, let's just cut the crap, shall we?'

A million emotions run through me throughout his speech, ranging from arousal to anger and shame, but I drink in every word he says, sitting upright. There is just something in his tone that makes me want to listen and obey. He clears his throat and I know that we are down to business now.

'We both know that I'm paying you, so you don't need to play nice. At least not yet. Please leave the acting to the guests at the party. Right now, I need your full attention. Is that clear?'

I nod, even though he can't see me. Then I roll my eyes at myself, because he can't see that, either.

'I didn't catch that.'

He says, voice a bit sterner, yet the velvety smoothness is still there. I think I should come up with a nickname for him, but that's only for the guys I really like, and I haven't made up my mind about Alec just yet.

'Yes, that's fine. So, what are the rules?'

I ask, even though I know most of them already. Alec's voice takes on a condescending undertone, one that's mostly reserved for naughty kids:

'Olivia, please. For someone who wants to be an actress, you aren't performing too well. Now listen to me, because the next part I won't tell you twice.'

I suppress a gasp, fear gripping me for a moment. He clearly knows more than I want him to, and yet here I am, knowing nothing about him. What have I done, selling myself to the highest bidder? He could even be a serial killer for all I know, hiring me for the night which I would never return from. Alec goes on, and it's becoming harder and harder to focus on his deceivingly sweet voice. At least he no longer talks to me as if I was a child, which is good I guess.

'There is a folder on the bed that contains every detail you need to know for tonight. It also contains the agreement we require you to sign.'

The word 'we' makes my head snap up, but I don't say a word. He continues, oblivious to my thumping heart and dry throat.

'Once you are done reading, there are certain items of clothing laid out for your on the chair next to the bed. You put them on, then get into the car that will be waiting by the front door at 8.30. Trust me, you don't want to be late, or our deal is off.'

I gulp, swallowing my shame. My cheeks are burning and I nod again. What did I expect? A romantic getaway, where the guy who bought me would pamper me? Please.

'Understood. Is there anything else I should know?'

Another sigh at the end of the line, then Alec's voice (the one he uses to make me shiver, and I'm pretty sure he does it on purpose) breaks through my rising panic:

'Yes. I have another proposition for you, but I will tell you more about that in the car. Now, please get ready, because you don't have much time left.'

I cringe at the words, but try to shut my emotions out. This is pure business, and there is a million bucks at the end of it. I can make sure my parents never struggle again, and I can even buy a house in Paris or somewhere else. Even the moon. I take in a deep breath before answering:

'Sounds good, I'm looking forward to it.'

Another moment of silence, but Alec must have noticed the tremble in my voice, because his silky smooth one darkens a shade when he speaks again:

'Olivia? Don't ever lie to me again. You don't want to know what I'm going to do to you if you do.'

And with that my throat closes up, my heart stops beating, and he hangs up. I'm left with the sound of the loud beep of the dead line and my deadlier thoughts. How the hell did this night go from sort-of-okay to outright poop? A 'helpful' voice inside my head reminds me that the twenty-four hours only starts once I sign the dotted line. And although a bigger part of me is scared shitless, the smaller part (the one that still needs the money, and also the one that's a tad bit curious as to the identity of the buyer) wins.

~o~

Kiss
&
Tell
Tail
Reverse Harem
Fairy Tales
1
Timea Tokes

Three
Policemen
&
Me
Reverse Harem
Chronicles
3
Timea Tokes

Other Books by Timea Tokes:

Paranormal Romance:
Her First Secret
Her Secret Admirer
His Secret Love
Their Last Secret
Her First And Last Secret Admirer

Erotic Short Stories:

Reverse Harem Chronicles:
Three Firemen & Me
Three Firemen & Me 2
Three Policemen & Me
Three Policemen & Me 2
Three Billionaires & Me

Reverse Harem Fairy Tales:
Kiss & Tell Tail
Kiss & Tell Tail 2

BDSM:
A Special Cup of Coffee – Pain and Pleasure

Hotwife:
Stuck & Shared

Holiday Erotica:
Mistletoe Boss
Dating The Author (Why Choose)
My Hitch-Hiking Valentine
The Bucket List
The Bucket List 2 - Damsel in Distress
Truth or Dare?

Exhibitionist & Voyeur:
Squirm Under My Watch
How About the Rooftop?
Don't Make A Sound

Paranormal Erotica:
Conjured Lover

The Plumber Series:
Seducing the Plumber 1: Sweet Time Waiting
Seducing the Plumber 2: Sweet Torture

The Escort Series:
The Escort's Taxi Ride
The Escort's Taxi Ride 2
The Escort's Taxi Ride 3

The Good Neighbor Series (Bisexual, Why Choose):
The Good Neighbor – An Unexpected Threesome
The Good Neighbor – Tied up by the Knight
The Good Neighbor – In the Backseat
The Good Neighbor – The Massage
The Good Neighbor – Guilty Pleasures

Sweet yet Naughty:
Forgotten
Blue Highlights

Gay:
The Stranger

Collections of Short Stories:
You Had Me At Kinky
You Had Me At Steamy
You Had Me At Rough

Coming Soon:

The Plumber's Excuse (2020)
Three Billionaires & Me (2020)
Kiss & Tell Tail 3 (2020)
A Cupid Mistake (2021)
Hell's Bride (2021)

Follow Timea Tokes on:

Amazon @timea_tokes

Twitter @timea_tokes

Facebook @herfirstsecret

Goodreads @timea_tokes

Sign up to her newsletter, and have a look at her blog for more bite-size erotica, paranormal romance, reviews and more:

www.timeatokes.com

<u>Note from the Author, Timea Tokes:</u>

~o~

My dear, lovely Reader, thank you for taking the time to read my story! I really hope you enjoyed it as much as I did writing it. As always, your feedback is highly valued and much appreciated.

Please do take the time to scroll to the end of the book and leave a review. It would mean the World to me!

And remember, this story is all about your pleasure.

On the next page, you can learn a bit more about me and why I write, but you will also find author interviews (and much more) on my website.

~o~

ABOUT THE AUTHOR

~o~

I have been writing short stories and poems since a young age, but my ultimate goal was creating a novel. Or a series, rather. Now, with my four paranormal romance novels published, as well as more than 30 erotica titles under my belt, , I think I can say that it came true - but this only fuels my desire to write more. After all, we are allowed to dream the same dream (over and over again) - and that's exactly what I'm planning to do :)

I enjoy helping people in any way possible, and I really hope that my books will prove to be inspirational in a way. Whether readers are looking for a swift (and steamy) erotic story, or a paranormal romance, I want them to associate themselves with my characters and realize stuff about themselves in the process.

Yes, even the bad things. Because, in life, there is no black and white, only colors. Therefore, I don't think any of my characters are either good or bad, but rather a little bit of both.

Aren't we all?

Well, if you never had guilty thoughts, never had any self-confidence issues, or if you never wanted something (or someone) who belonged to someone else, then probably my books won't be for you. But, who knows, I might be able to show you a different perspective. I like to experiment with different genres, and new concepts and ideas.

I really enjoy learning as much as I can about people, what makes them tick (and live, laugh, cry, and sigh). In fact, I think our World (and those beyond) are so diverse, ten thousand lifetimes wouldn't be enough to explore it all. But one thing I truly believe in: those who belong in your life will find a way there. Therefore my stories are usually based on chance encounters and ordinary events that take an unexpected turn.

Like a blind date on Valentine's day, or a haircut, or a new job. Who says you can't meet someone 'accidentally'; while going to the hairdresser, someone you lost contact with 500 years ago? Trust me, you can. You just need to brace every day (and every book) with open eyes - and an open heart.

Just remember: my stories are all about you, and you alone. If they capture your attention (and your heart), then I've done my 'job'. I regularly try to release new content, both on Amazon and my blog. Please feel free to have a look, and sign up to my newsletter.

And, just so you know: I care about your opinion, very much so. Whether you liked my work or you didn't, I would be honored if you let me know what it meant for you. It would mean the world to me!

~o~

1. *When did you create your first erotica story, and what was it about?*

Well, my first story wasn't fully erotica, more a romance story. In fact, I never thought that one day I would write anything steamy. Not at all. I was shy, and grew up in an environment, where everything was taboo. Sharing my views on sex with anyone, let alone write about it? No way…

And yet, I soon had to realize that writing romantic stories couldn't happen without the couple getting it on eventually. Especially because the first four books series I created was about the same characters, and they are 100 pages each (which is a lot to go without including a sex scene every now and again). I must admit, I delayed the inevitable for as long as I could, just to realize later how much I enjoyed writing about sex.

Although my first attempts were very timid indeed, I tried to avoid being too explicit or descriptive. I concentrated on the romantic and paranormal aspect of it (the main characters dream about each other, and somehow when I was writing about the dreams, they gave me courage to be a bit braver).

But it wasn't until I started writing my erotic short stories in 2015, when I started to experiment. Well, if you have a look at 'The Good Neighbour', you can see how my explicitness and mood changed throughout the series.

I think I can say that this was the very first fully erotic story I created, fulfilling one of my secret fantasies (no, I don't have a hot neighbour, or at least I don't think I have, but the idea always fascinated me).

2. *What (or who) inspired you to start writing erotica?*

My own lack of courage, if I'm honest. All my friends were so open about their relationships and their fantasies, so I thought:

"Why do I have to be this way, when I want to explore everything that's out there?"

And as I have always enjoyed writing, I decided to try it out on paper. It started as a therapy I prescribed for myself, and then it escalated, taking me to places I never thought I would visit. I must say that I'm really glad I gave in to temptation.

3. *What do you find most challenging when writing these stories?*

To let them go when I finish writing them. I believe that it isn't possible, especially when I create a longer story. The characters, the feelings stay with me long after, as they become part of me for at least a little while.

Another aspect of it is that I keep thinking about what others read into them, and whether they convey their meaning in a way that I intended them to. But, just like when you give birth to a child, when writing a story as well you need to give it space after some time.

I once read a quotation (not sure where, or who said it, but it made me smile and I could definitely relate):

"I met the man of my dreams last night.. in chapter five..." *Sigh*

4. Do you write in other genres, and if yes, then would you consider mixing them with erotica?

Yes, and not sure. I ghost-write for a living, as well as create my own stories, which include romance, horror, thriller, fantasy, crime and more, but I'm not sure it would feel right to mix them with erotica. Mind that, I have had some strange requests that were a mixture, like fetish-horror, but it didn't actually include erotica. I suppose it could have, as it was about a foot fetish, which seems to be quite popular. Oh well, another thing to look at in the future :)

My favourite ones are psychological thrillers though, so I could probably turn one of those into erotica, but at the moment I'm thinking of a transition, rather than a mix. So, for example it would start as a thriller, but have a sexual ending. Hmm...

5. Have you written any stories that were inspired by real life events?

Yes. In fact, my very first story, 'Her First and Last Secret Admirer' (the four books I mentioned earlier) started with an actual recurring medieval dream, which I then implemented into the plot, creating a story and background for it. If it wasn't for that urge to put the whole thing into writing, I probably would never have picked up the courage to write at all. Now it is both in print and on Kindle, so I guess it was a nice bargain :)

I think that writing about real events, twisting them a little, but still keeping them close to your heart is an important process.

Also, that way you can relive those events over and over again, and others will keep guessing what was the real part in it.

Strangely enough, it adds to its mystery (and excitement, of course)...

6. *What is your speciality and why?*

I would say it's mixing the past with the present. I'm not an expert, but I also love to keep up the suspense until the end. Although this doesn't always come through in my erotic stories, as they are linear, but in my paranormal romance books, I draw a parallel between what happened 500 years ago and what's happening right now. It's difficult to explain without revealing the plot itself, but I do love to play with the mind of the reader, if you know what I mean.

7. *Are there any topics you don`t like writing about?*

Now? Not really. If you asked me a few years ago, I would have said everything that involves sex ;)

I guess I just realized that I shouldn't say no, just because I don't know how something feels. If I don't try it, I will never know... If I'm not familiar with a topic, then

I do my research, but not too many things scare me nowadays (without wanting to sound weird or vain).

8. *Do you have any tips / warnings for newbie erotica writers?*

Follow your dreams. You will get some ugly feedback (or none at all), but that doesn't mean that your work isn't appreciated. Don't take them personally, but accept them, so that they can serve as stepping stones, helping you improve your writing. We all make mistakes; that's what makes us human.

Personally, I couldn't wait to grab a physical copy of my books, and that made up for whatever negativity I got (but luckily it has only been minor stuff so far).

So, if you are thinking about writing, or if you already have a story or two, try to make them into a book, no matter how tiny it is. Trust me, as soon as you have it on your shelf, you will become a different person.

9. *What is your favourite season and why?*

Spring, because that's when everything comes to life. I just love to watch the flowers blossom and the world wake up from its winter slumber. I always feel like I'm reborn myself every time springs comes (I know, I'm a hopeless romantic).